A GOLDEN BOOK • NEW YORK

Library of Congress Control Number: 2008933820
www.goldenbooks.com
www.randomhouse.com/kids
ISBN: 978-0-7364-2587-2
MANUFACTURED IN SINGAPORE
10 9 8 7 6 5 4 3 2 1
First Random House Edition 2009

Now, most of you who are reading this book probably live above the sea . . .

. . . but others live underwater.

Nemo and his father, Marlin, lived underwater. They were clownfish.

Because they were clownfish,
they were small. But other fish
were big!

Marlin was scared of the big
fish, so he always kept Nemo
close to him, tucked safely
inside their little home.

But today was Nemo's first day of school!
He was very excited. On the way there he saw . . .

a spotted fish . . .

. . . and a striped fish.

He saw *angry* fish . . .

. . . and HAPPY fish.

Mr. Ray, the science teacher, took
Nemo's class on a field trip. Nemo
and his friends sneaked away and
swam to the really deep water.
Marlin chased after Nemo and
scolded him! Nemo was angry that
his father had embarrassed him in
front of his new friends . . .

. . . so he swam

. . . and swam

. . . and swam

way up to the surface
of the ocean until he
touched a boat!

Then Nemo got caught!

"Daddy!" cried Nemo.

"Nemo!" cried Marlin.

Nemo was taken away in the boat. Marlin
tried to save his son, but the boat sped away
so fast it soon disappeared. Nemo was gone.
But Marlin would not give up. The only thing
on his mind now was finding Nemo.

Looking for help, Marlin swam into all sorts of fish. They pushed him and shoved him. They bumped into him. Soon Marlin was knocked aside.

One friendly fish named Dory swam down to
see if Marlin was okay. She was a little bit silly,
and she couldn't remember very much, but
she was happy to help Marlin!

Together, Dory and Marlin met a shark. Marlin was scared! But Dory thought it was very nice of the shark to invite them to a party.

The party was for sharks who were trying not to eat fish. Luckily, they did not eat Marlin and Dory.

Marlin kept searching for
Nemo. He and Dory found a
scuba mask that belonged to the
diver who had taken Nemo. They
swam down into a very deep,
dark place to get it.

Then they saw a light.

The light was attached to a mean anglerfish!
But it helped Dory read an address written on the
mask. Then the two friends swam away before
the anglerfish could eat them! Now Marlin knew
where to find Nemo: 42 Wallaby Way, Sydney.
Dory was so excited that she repeated the address
over and over . . . and over.

Next Marlin and Dory met some moonfish.
The moonfish made funny shapes.

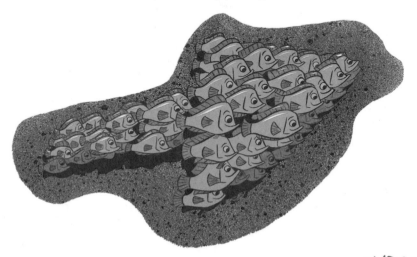

They pointed toward 42 WALLABY WAY, SYDNEY

Some friendly
turtles gave Marlin and Dory a ride.

Marlin told the
story of his search
for Nemo, and the
news spread across
the ocean!

Even Nemo heard about it at 42 Wallaby Way, Sydney. He was very excited! He wanted to escape from the fish tank where he was trapped.

Nemo's new friends were excited, too. The little clownfish was bursting with pride. He had the bravest dad in the sea!

Then a whale swallowed Marlin and Dory!
Dory told Marlin he didn't need to worry.
And she was right. The whale took them
as close as he could get to 42 Wallaby Way,
Sydney. In fact, he took them all the way to

Sydney Harbor!

At last a pelican named
Nigel helped Marlin and Dory
go straight to 42 Wallaby Way,
Sydney. But it was too late.
A little girl had grabbed Nemo.
Marlin couldn't save him!

Marlin was sad. He thought he would never see his son again.

But Nemo had escaped! Dory found him.

Father and son were overjoyed.

And when they finally returned home, both Nemo and Marlin were heroes.

Lightning McQueen was a race car! He was *flashy* red and had a **SHINY** lightning bolt on his side.

He even had adoring fans.
But he also had a **BiG** problem.
His pit crews kept quitting. You see,
Lightning thought he could do
everything by himself.

And since all Lightning
cared about was winning races,
he didn't have any friends . . .

except **Mack**.

Mack the truck drove Lightning to all his races. One night, Lightning wanted to get to a **really BiG** race really fast. He made Mack drive too long, and the loyal truck got **tired**.

Mack swerved, and Lightning fell out the back of the truck! **Uh-oh!**

Lightning had been sleeping.
But he woke up fast! The race car
was **LOST** and *scared*!

Soon he was
racing toward an
old forgotten
town called
**Radiator
Springs**.

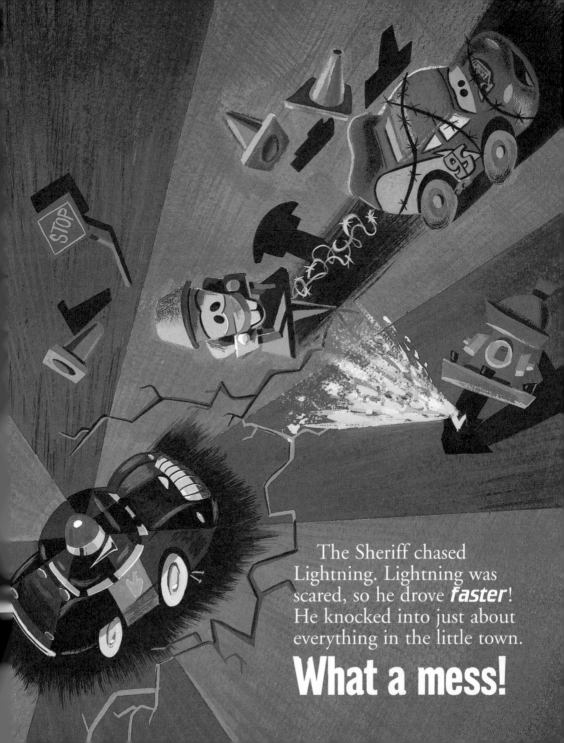

The Sheriff chased
Lightning. Lightning was
scared, so he drove *faster*!
He knocked into just about
everything in the little town.

What a mess!

When the chase was over, Lightning had ruined the town's main street. He was in a heap of **trouble**.

In fact, the Sheriff had him towed to jail for all the damage he had done.

Only one car in town was friendly to Lightning—
a rusty tow truck named Mater. Mater didn't know
that Lightning was a famous car. He just wanted to
make a new **friend**.

Soon Lightning was brought to court. He thought he would be set free because he was **a superstar race car**.

He was right—almost. Doc, the town's judge, told Lightning to leave town and never come back. He didn't like race cars.

Then Sally, a blue sports car, arrived. She was a lawyer. Lightning thought Sally was pretty.

But Sally just wanted Lightning to fix the mess he had made.

The townsfolk agreed. They loved their town. So Sally and Doc made a deal: Lightning could leave **AFTER** he fixed the road.

Accused

But Lightning was still in a rush to get to his big race. So he worked too fast and made an even **BIGGER** mess of the messy road.

A little while later, the town watched as Mater tried to drive on the new road. But the road was simply too **BUMPY**.

Doc was angry. He challenged Lightning to a race. "If you win, you go and I fix the road," said Doc. "If I win, you do the road **MY** way."

It certainly looked as if
Lightning would win the race.
But he didn't. He crashed into a
cactus patch. Luckily, his new
friend, Mater, helped
him out.

After that, Lightning McQueen learned a few things.

He learned that the townsfolk were **proud** of their home.

He learned why Sally **loved** Radiator Springs.

And he learned that Doc had once been a ***champion*** race car

Finally, Lightning fixed the road. Then he thanked all his new friends by getting spiffed up—Radiator Springs style!

Red the fire truck squirted **Lightning clean.**

Guido and Luigi gave him new **tires.**

Ramone gave
him a new
paint job.

And Flo gave
him a can of her
best oil.

By that night,
the townsfolk had
fixed their shops
and their **NEON** lights!
The **OLD** town looked
NEW again!

Soon it was time to
go back to the racetrack.
But now Lightning had
Doc as his crew chief.
He also had a new pit
crew. And they weren't
just his teammates—
they were his new
best friends.

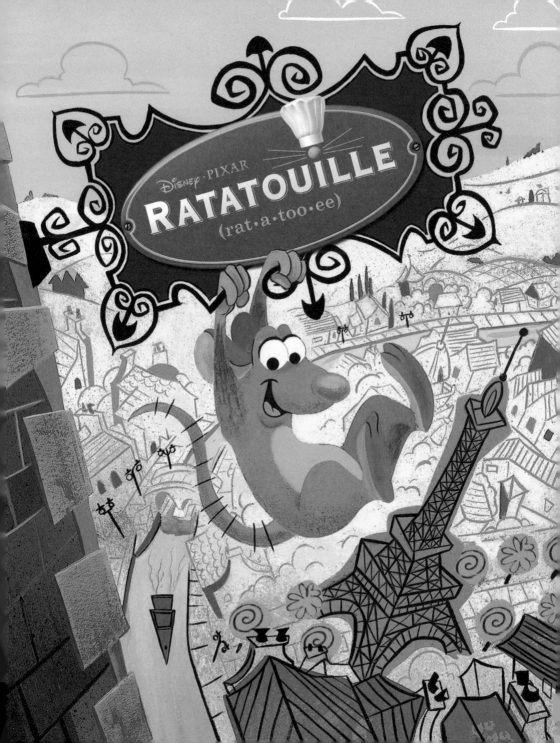

This is
the story
of Remy,
a little rat
with

BIG

dreams.

Remy wasn't like all the other rats. For one thing, he had an extraordinary sense of

SMELL.

He also had a taste for finer food.

And *THAT* is why Remy dreamed of being . . .
a *CHEF!*

But Django,
Remy's father,
had another
job for him . . .

. . . poison checker. The compost heap was where
the rats got all their food. Remy had the
important job of sorting the safe garbage from the
bad garbage. This was NOT part of his dream.

One day,
the rats had to flee
their home. A **HUMAN**
had discovered them!
As the human chased them,
the rats ran to their
ESCAPE boats and
floated into
the sewers.

Remy got separated from the others
and ended up near a fancy French
restaurant—in

PARIS.

The restaurant used to belong to Remy's idol,
the late and great chef, Auguste Gusteau.
Now Gusteau popped up in Remy's
IMAGINATION.
Then—whoops!

Remy fell from
the skylight into
the kitchen.

The restaurant
was an EXCITING place
for Remy, but it was
SCARY, too.

In the kitchen, Remy cooked a pot of soup to replace what the garbage boy had spilled. The garbage boy was named Linguini. After that, Linguini and Remy became friends. *AND* they were a secret cooking team.

SHHHH!

Meanwhile, Django and the rest of the
rat colony made a new home in the dark,
wet sewers under Paris. Things weren't
the same without Remy. Django
kept hoping he would
find his son one day.

But Remy was happy. He did miss his family, but he had found his place in the world. Working together, Linguini and Remy made great food, even though Remy had to stay hidden. The human chefs did not want a rat in their kitchen!

Once, after cooking a wonderful meal, the chefs celebrated in the kitchen. Remy celebrated, too, in the back alley, where . . .

. . . he found his brother EMILE!

Emile took Remy **HOME**
to the rats' new colony
in the sewer.

Of course, Django was HAPPY to see Remy again!

But Remy didn't feel as if he belonged with the rats anymore. He didn't want to go back to smelling garbage.

"I have friends, a place to live, work that I love," Remy tried to explain to his dad. "I'll come back often," he said. But for now he had to return to his new home and the restaurant. Remy's dad didn't understand.

Remy went back to being a little chef. Meanwhile, Linguini was falling in LOVE!

Soon Linguini found out that he was the owner of the restaurant! And the restaurant was becoming very famous. Linguini enjoyed the attention.

Linguini decided he didn't need Remy anymore.
They
ARGUED.

Remy felt very
SAD
and
ALONE.

Who was his
family now?

But Linguini needed **HELP.**

He had to cook a special dinner for a special guest. And Linguini told Remy he was SORRY. *UH-OH!* The other chefs didn't like rats, so they left.

Django saw
Linguini being kind
to Remy.
He asked everyone
in the rat colony to
pitch in to help make
the special dinner.
All the rats became
little chefs!

With the rats' help,
the meal was a success.
The SPECIAL dish was
ratatouille!

The rats also helped Remy **CHASE** away the health inspector . . .

. . . who still **CLOSED** the restaurant for having rats.

LA RATATOUILLE

That gave Remy and his friends an idea. They opened a **NEW** one!

And Remy's colony ate at the restaurant, too—enjoying all the fine food they could ever want.

Menu

Best of all, Remy became a chef at last.

"I am PROUD of you no matter what," Django said.